W9-BZA-522

MY HOUSE IS ALIVE!

THE WEIRD AND WONDERFUL SOUNDS YOUR HOUSE MAKES

Thank you, Sheila, for wondering
what's behind the walls!
—SR

MY HOUSE IS ALIVE!

THE WEIRD AND WONDERFUL SOUNDS YOUR HOUSE MAKES

Scot Ritchie

Owlkids Books

WITHDRAWN

VAN
E
RIT

16.95

Have you ever noticed
there are some noises
you only hear at night?

Who's that at the door?

That knocking sound is made by
metal expanding and contracting.
Metal vents carry warm air to
heat your home. When metal heats
up, it expands, and when it cools
down, it shrinks.

THUMP, BANG, BOOM!

There's nobody else home...What's that sound in the bathroom?

It's just the toilet running. A toilet tank has a drain with a plug in it called a *flapper*. When the flapper is loose, the water leaks down the drain between flushes. This is what makes that gurgling, trickling noise.

Can you hear
that watery
noise?

Refrigerators make lots of noises, but if you hear trickling water, it could be the defroster at work. The defroster's job is to melt ice. The water runs down a drain inside the fridge...

TRICKLE, DRIP!

BUZZZZZZ....

What's that buzzing noise?

Fluorescent lights often make noise. Inside the light box is something called a ballast. The ballast is made of metal plates that store energy. Sometimes there is so much energy, the metal plates vibrate — *BUZZz!*

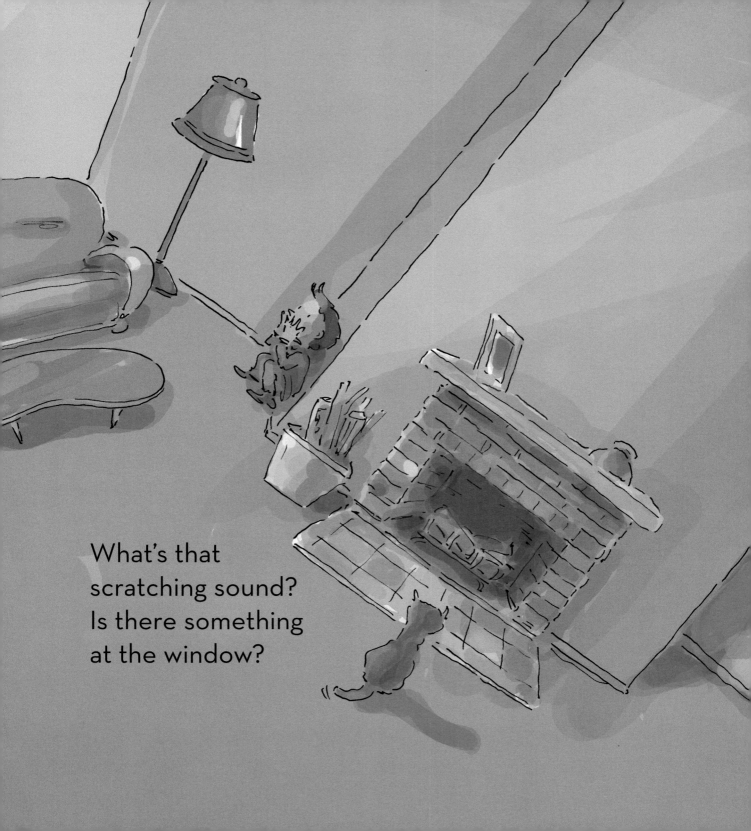

What's that
scratching sound?
Is there something
at the window?

If the chimney isn't being used, birds might think it's a safe place to nest. The sounds you hear are the birds bringing in twigs or scratching the bricks. If the birds like their chimney nest, they might even lay eggs there!

Something is making a noise, but nobody's upstairs...

Wood is often shipped in open railroad cars, where it can get soaked with rain. The water makes the wood expand. When the wood is brought into a new house and used to build stairs, it starts to dry out. As the wood dries, it shrinks — and creaks!

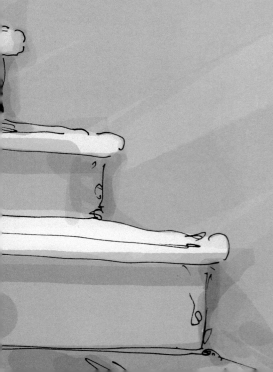

What is that crunching noise?
It's something big!

CRUUUNCH!

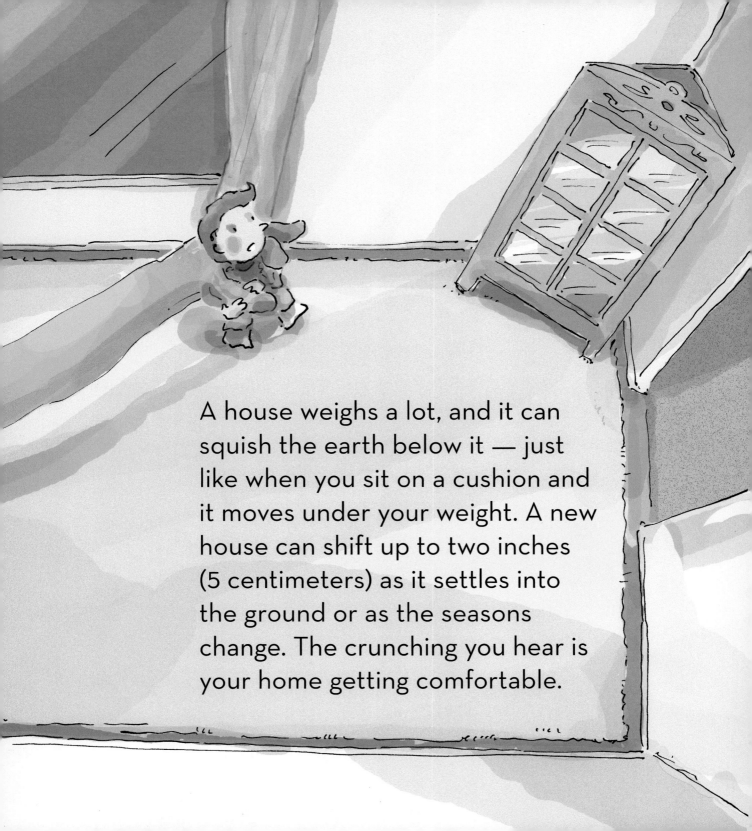

A house weighs a lot, and it can squish the earth below it — just like when you sit on a cushion and it moves under your weight. A new house can shift up to two inches (5 centimeters) as it settles into the ground or as the seasons change. The crunching you hear is your home getting comfortable.

What is that hair-raising sound?

The garage door can make a lot of noise. The door's motor is attached to a chain. It pulls the chain one way to open the door and the other way to close it. Push a button and — *presto* — the door rumbles open!

Houses make all sorts of sounds at night. Here's one more you might know...

YAWWWWWN!

Text and illustrations © 2016 Scot Ritchie

All rights reserved. No part of this publication may be reproduced, stored in a retrieval system, or transmitted in any form or by any means, without the prior written permission of Owlkids Books Inc., or in the case of photocopying or other reprographic copying, a license from the Canadian Copyright Licensing Agency (Access Copyright). For an Access Copyright license, visit www.accesscopyright.ca or call toll-free to 1-800-893-5777.

Owlkids Books acknowledges the financial support of the Canada Council for the Arts, the Ontario Arts Council, the Government of Canada through the Canada Book Fund (CBF) and the Government of Ontario through the Ontario Media Development Corporation's Book Initiative for our publishing activities.

Published in Canada by
Owlkids Books Inc.
10 Lower Spadina Avenue
Toronto, ON M5V 2Z2

Published in the United States by
Owlkids Books Inc.
1700 Fourth Street
Berkeley, CA 94710

Cataloguing data available from Library and Archives Canada

ISBN 978-1-77147-136-7

Library of Congress Control Number: 2015947586

The artwork in this book was rendered in Adobe Photoshop.
Edited by: Jessica Burgess
Designed by: Claudia Dávila
Consultant: Dana Murchison

Canada Council for the Arts Conseil des Arts du Canada

ONTARIO ARTS COUNCIL
CONSEIL DES ARTS DE L'ONTARIO
an Ontario government agency
un organisme du gouvernement de l'Ontario

Manufactured in Shenzhen, Guangdong, China, in September 2015, by WKT Co. Ltd.
Job #15CB1181

A   B   C   D   E   F

Selected Sources

Mitchell Parker, "What's That Sound? 9 Home Noises and How to Fix Them," Houzz, www.houzz.com/ideabooks.

Shannon Lee, "5 Strange House Noises Explained," Improvement Center, www.improvementcenter.com.

"Troubleshooting a Furnace Duct: Banging Noises," Do It Yourself, www.doityourself.com.

"What's That Noise in My Attic!" Pest Control Answers, Treatments and Solutions, May 3, 2010, www.bugspray.net.

Yvan Cazabon, "Why Does My House Make Loud Cracking Sounds in Very Cold Weather?" *Carleton Now*, carletonnow.carleton.ca/February-2005.

 Publisher of Chirp, chickaDEE and OWL
www.owlkidsbooks.com

Owlkids Books is a division of Bayard
CANADA